WATC
TRICERATOPS!

based on text by Dawn Bentley
Illustrated by Karen Carr

Little®
Soundprints

For Aiden Nicolas. Love, Aunt Dawn. — D.B.

Dedicated with best wishes and love to Don, Tena and Dylan Borchert. — K.C.

Published by Soundprints Division of Trudy Corporation, Norwalk, Connecticut.

Book design: Marcin Pilchowski
Editor: Laura Gates Galvin
Editorial assistance: Brian E. Giblin

First Edition 2004
10 9 8 7 6 5 4 3
Printed in China

Acknowledgements:
      Our very special thanks to Dr. Brett-Surman of the Smithsonian Institution's National Museum of Natural History.
      Soundprints would also like to thank Ellen Nanney and Katie Mann of the Smithsonian Institution for their help in the creation of this book.

*Library of Congress Cataloging-in-Publication Data is
on file with the publisher and the Library of Congress.*

WATCH OUT,
TRICERATOPS!

based on text by Dawn Bentley

Illustrated by Karen Carr

A note to the reader:
Throughout this story you will see words in **bold letters**.
There is more information about these words in the
glossary. The glossary is in the back of the book.

One sunny day
a Triceratops and
his **herd** set out
to look for food.

Triceratops hears a

noise in the trees.

He sneaks up for

a closer look. Two

Pachycephalosaurus

are fighting.

Sun shines on the **ferns** below. Triceratops loves to eat ferns! He breaks off a stem and chews it.

Triceratops eats until he is full. He looks up. His herd is not with him! He is not safe alone.

Flying reptiles circle above Triceratops. Triceratops runs and hides. The flying reptiles find something else on the ground.

Triceratops rests in the shade. Suddenly, two eyes stare down at him. It is a hungry **Tyrannosaurus rex**!

Tyrannosaurus rex
is a meat eater.
She has lots of
big, sharp teeth!

Tyrannosaurus rex is hungry. Triceratops would make a tasty meal for her!

Triceratops is smaller than Tyrannosaurus rex. But he can use his **horns** to fight. Suddenly, the ground shakes!

It is Triceratops' herd!
They are here to help
him. Tyrannosaurus
rex cannot win this
fight. She stomps away.

Triceratops is safe again. Triceratops is also hungry again! He and his herd look for more plants to eat.

Glossary

Herd: A large number of animals of the same kind that travel as a group.

Horns: Hard, pointed projections on animals, reptiles, birds, fish, or insects.

Fern: A plant that has roots, stems and fronds, but no flowers.

Tyrannosaurus rex: *Tyrannosaurus rex* was the biggest meat-eating dinosaur that ever lived on land.

Pachycephalosaurus: A dinosaur with a very thick skull. The males may have had head-butting contests.

ABOUT THE *TRICERATOPS*
(try-SAIR-uh-tops)

Triceratops lived on earth about 65 million years ago! *Triceratops* means "three-horned face." All *Triceratops* had horns. Their big horns and bony neck shields would scare some enemies and protect them from others.

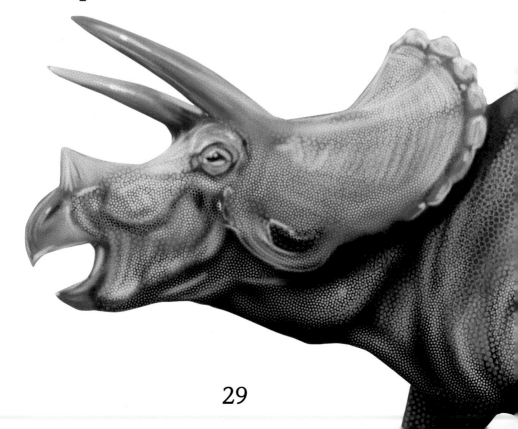

Triceratops was the biggest and heaviest of the horned dinosaurs. It weighed 11 tons and was nearly 30 feet long!

Triceratops was a plant-eater and had a strong, sharp beak that helped it bite through thick stems and branches.

Other dinosaurs that lived with Triceratops:

Pachycephalosaurus (PAK-i-SEF-a-lo-SAWR-us)

Parasaurolophus (PAR-a-saw-ROL-o-fus)

Quetzalcoatlus (KWET-sal-coh-AT-lus)

Tyrannosaurus rex (tye-RAN-oh-saur-us rex)